Petey and the Bee
A Dog's Tale

Rebecca and James McDonald

HOUSE OF LORE

Petey and the Bee

ISBN: 978-0-9886598-5-8

www.HouseofLore.net

First House of Lore paperback edition, 2013

Book Website
www.SamiAndThomas.com

It was a sunny day in Cottage Cove. Vesters the cat was leaning against the bottom of a tree, keeping an eye on Petey the dog. Petey was slowly sniffing his way around the backyard while Sami and Thomas were helping their mom and dad build a tree house.

With everyone busy working, Petey was getting bored. He tried to climb the ladder to the tree house so he could help the family, but he only managed to fall on his back and get laughed at by Vesters.

Like most dogs, Petey loved to play ball. He begged Vesters to play toss, but it all came to an angry end when the ball landed in the middle of the birdbath, soaking Vesters (who hated to be wet) and putting the toy just out of reach of Petey's sniffing nose.

So Petey wandered, sniffing his way into the far corner of the backyard where the flowers grew wild and the grass grew thick and tall.

With the warm sun on his back and the sweet smell of wild flowers, Petey couldn't help but dive into a thick patch of grass and roll. He rubbed his back against the ground and kicked up grass and flowers everywhere.

What Petey didn't realize was one of the flowers he'd sent flying through the air had a plump, fuzzy bee on it. The bee happened to be named Charlie, and he didn't like to be disturbed while working.

Charlie the bee wiggled his way out from under the torn up grass and flowers. He flew up high to get a good look at what had just upset his warm and sunny day. That's when he spotted Petey twisting and snorting in a swirl of flowers and grass. Instead of thinking things through calmly, Charlie readied his stinger, and pointed it straight at the furry backside of the playful dog.

When Petey came to his feet, he gave a big shake from head to tail to get the loose grass off. He had no idea the trouble that was brewing just above him.

Charlie swooped down landing his stinger right into the very tip of Petey's tail, sending Petey yelping into the air.

Petey's tail felt like it was on fire, and it was starting to swell. All he could do to get away from the pain was run. Vesters the cat rushed over to see what happened to his old pal but couldn't figure out why Petey looked like he was trying to get away from his own tail.

Petey went spinning past, bumping into Vesters and sending him flying into the middle of the birdbath.

In the meantime, Charlie the bee went to sit on a fence post and straighten his bent stinger. He was surprised that the furry tip of a dog's tail could be so hard underneath.

What Charlie didn't see was the bluebird swooping down from behind, ready to eat him for lunch.

Just as Charlie looked up and saw the wide open beak coming straight at him, Petey bumped into the fence post, trying to nip the end of his very sore tail.

Charlie went flying safely into a bush and the bird swooped back into the sky, startled by the frantic dog and unable to make Charlie his meal.

When Charlie finally found his way out of the bush, he was so happy that Petey had saved him from being eaten that he wanted to meet this newfound friend. He dusted himself off and flew up high to locate where the fast and furry hero had disappeared to.

Across the yard, Vesters the cat was shaking off his soaking wet fur. When he saw the swollen tip of Petey's tail, he felt sorry for his friend and wanted to help. So Vesters fished the ball out of the birdbath, hoping a game of toss would get Petey to forget his hurt tail.

In no time, Petey was so busy playing with Vesters he forgot all about the pain.

But one thing Petey couldn't figure out was why a big yellow bee kept landing on his nose, buzzing and humming, almost like he was trying to say something.

Read All The
Sami and Thomas
Stories

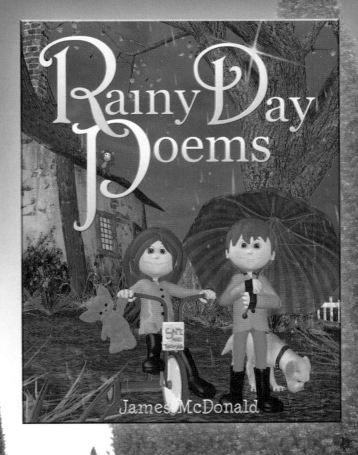

Rainy Day Poems

James McDonald

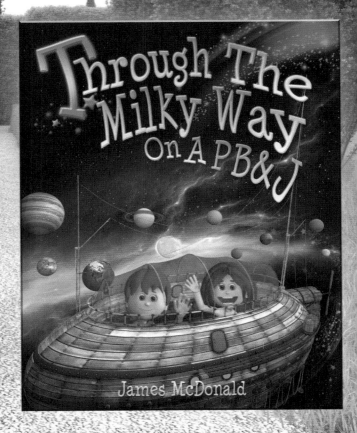

Through The Milky Way On A PB&J

James McDonald